ROUND

Written by S. R. Taylor

Illustrated by Dayne Sislen and Charity Russell

and when her grandmother ♪
said her name
♪ Olivia
Catherine
Amanda
Mae
Brown
♫ The sound became music
and came out round. ♪

To
Michael,
Marlin,
Athena…
who truly believed
I had wings
and told me to fly.

'ROUND'
The story of a little girl who learned to believe in herself.

By S.R. Taylor
Illustrated by Dayne Sislen and Charity Russell
Composition by Mary McNitt and Nikkita Cohoon

Printed by
McNaughton & Gunn

ISBN 978-1-940786-12-4

Foreword

I grew up feeling a little different than other kids. I was younger (as a result of skipping 1st grade), wore glasses, had crazy curly hair, and I was about 10 pounds heavier than most of the girls. I was called mixed-girl, nerd, four-eyes, and excluded from "popular girl" games on the playground. I can still remember walking around during recess all by myself. To combat the alienation, I made it a habit to go into the library during lunchtime. That way, I felt, no one would see me by myself. After school, I couldn't wait to get home and tell my mother about my day just to hear her tell me I was precious, beautiful, and it was okay to be smart and it was okay to be different and to be myself no matter what. I can honestly say, because of those conversations, I was able to walk into the classroom every day, knowing I wasn't like everyone else, and truly being okay with that…being okay with being me.

Now I wish I could say that things got better for me as I got older, that once I started middle school and then high school, my situation changed, and that I had a plethora of friends, and everything was perfect. What changed for me was not my situation, but how I looked at it and how I reacted. The words my mother said to me resonated throughout my mind, day in and day out, ultimately becoming my own thoughts about myself. These thoughts served as motivation, and ultimately propelled me to do things I wouldn't have been able to do otherwise.

I competed in (and won) beauty pageants, completed graduate school, began a mentoring group, and I'm currently pursuing my PhD.

I credit all that I've done, and all that I will do, to the constant motivation and unwavering encouragement of my mother. Those daily conversations with her reminded me that it was indeed okay to be different, and that being different in no way minimizes my awesomeness. With her love, I continued to push past the stares, pointed fingers, and taunting done by so many students. I chose to love me—my skin, body, hair and all.

So I write this to thank my mother for listening to me—my complaints, my stories and my crying—from years and years of bullying. She never once acted uninterested or unsupportive. I thank her for her daily reminders of how strong I was, despite how weak I felt inside. I thank her for her courage as a single mother, not letting her own stresses take away from what she built inside of me as a young woman. And where it started, was in a young, awkwardly feeling little girl much like the character in *ROUND*. So I invite you to get to know me, through the eyes of adorable Olivia Catherine Amanda Mae Brown.

—Athena

Simply put, Olivia was round.
Named after almost every
woman in her family,

Olivia
Catherine
Amanda
Mae Brown

really should've worn her
name like a crown.

But Olivia was sad.
Poor Olivia felt bad. Soon
she would see there was
so much more
in her to be found
than simply
the nickname
ROUND.

LAW THREE:
No one's better than me.

LAW TWO:
Everyone wants to be me.

LAW ONE:
I'm brighter than the sun.

One morning at school, she peeked over her shoulder and paused noticing three mean girls discussing their three mean girl laws.

She tiptoed past them pretending to be brave. All the while she looked for her desk—her secret hideaway.

"Attention! Attention!"

The teacher Ms. Chimes announced.

Our class has been chosen
to put on a play,
'The Backyard Ballet.'
 "Does anyone want to be
a flower, a tree, a bird
or bumblebee?"
 "I want to be a spider!"
exclaimed wiggly Ryder.
 "Can I be a bunny?"
squealed a hopping Sunny.

Scanning the room and adjusting her glasses,
Ms. Chimes suddenly noticed little girl raising
her hand as slow as molasses.
  "Miss Olivia," she said, checking off names,
"have you decided what part you would like to play?"
  Olivia waited. And waited some more.
Then she looked out the window. Then down at the floor.
  She looked at Ms. Chimes and at the children once more.
She even looked at the cobweb hanging over the door.

Butterfly

"I want to be a butterfly."

"We are the butterflies!" the mean girls meanly cried. "You're too big. You're too wide. There are no butterflies your size," Tia, the queen of the meanies replied.

"That's enough," said Ms. Chimes firmly, "We don't want anyone wearing a frown. There's room for one more butterfly, especially one as pretty as Miss Olivia Brown."

The bell rang, and Olivia's classmates happily sang while running happily out the door, leaving Olivia in the classroom with only her shadow and nothing more. Even the spider took his cobweb dragging it gently across the floor.

Olivia heard the children laughing even after they had all gone, until finally she arrived at her Grandma Octavia's cottage on the corner of Ivy and Long.

"How was school today Libby?"
asked Grandma Octavia.
"Did you learn something new?
What wonderful things did you
wonderfully do?"

"Grandma, I want to be a
butterfly, but they said I'm
too round to be dancing or
flying high off the ground."
"Olivia, your mommy was
round when she was your age.
It never stopped her from
dancing on that stage.
If you want to be a butterfly,
you must be brave."

Joining their fingers and holding them tight, Olivia and her grandmother **twirled** and **whirled** with all their might.

Falling down dizzy, they let out a big laugh as they **wiggled** and **giggled** on top of the grass.

Flapping their arms they made cherry blossom angels
and lay on their backs smiling and watching flower
petals **dangle**.

"Now this is a real backyard ballet," Olivia said
watching her grandmother spread her wings and play.

Later that night, Olivia said her prayers.
"*Protect me as you would the apple of your eye. Let me know what they say is a lie. Hide me under the shadow of your wings.*"

When the house was all quiet—except for the wind through the trees, Oscar the dog snoring and buzzing bees—Olivia dreamed of truly extraordinary things. She saw a beautiful butterfly flutter and zoom, swirling and twirling in her room.

"Your name is Olivia!" said the butterfly with pride, writing her name in the air with the light from the fireflies. "Olivia Catherine Amanda Mae Brown—your name's indeed on the top of my list." The butterfly smiled and gave her a big butterfly kiss.

"What list?" Olivia asked, with both hands on her hips.
"No time for that Olivia, for stupdendous,

momentous

things are bound
to be found
in such a pretty
little girl that
happens to be
round!"

"Now dance like no one's looking,

laugh out loud and close your eyes.

You'll feel yourself *Rise*

and find your wings
from the joy cocooned inside."

Without any warning or even a sound, do you know what Olivia Catherine Amanda Mae found?

The little girl discovered a bright golden crown on top of her head, and a pair of butterfly wings much like the butterfly said.

Early the next morning, as the sun was set to rise—
Olivia awoke to the smell of tea cakes, the sound of
laughter and a very special surprise.

It was even better than her dream, Olivia's beautiful
patchwork wings made of pieces of her aunts' favorite
things.

Aunt Catherine sewed the word COURAGE. Aunt
Amanda stitched the word FAITH. Grandma added JOY.
Aunt Mae covered the wings with GRACE.

They added pearls, buttons and lace.
Drank honey bush tea and ate tea
cakes. Olivia fluttered and played in
her very own backyard ballet.

And when Monday morning came, she quickly rushed out the door. She didn't notice she'd left her wings right there on the kitchen floor.

"Attention! Attention!"

Ms. Chimes began, "We are picking the parts for the play. I hope you're ready! Auditions are today."

"Me first! Me first!" shouted the mean girls unrehearsed.

But just as they were quickly moving, pushing and shoving their classmates meanly, Nia suddenly noticed Olivia unexpectedly beaming, causing her to stumble into a screaming Mia who then tumbled into Tia.

Such a disaster, caused Ms. Chimes to turnabout—quite astonished by the mean girls, and their truly mean girl shouts.

"It was stupid Ryder's spider bringing everything to a halt!"

"Nooooo it's stupid Sunny, and her four-eyed bunny's fault!"

"You three come with me," said Ms. Chimes most quietly. Then with a big smile, "Everyone deserves a chance to dance! Olivia, are you ready to show us your butterfly prance?"
And do you know what happened next?

Olivia smiled back, and before she could answer, her classmates shouted,

"Yes!"

Olivia practiced until the day of the play—

dancing and spinning and whirling about—

prancing and twirling with her hands lifted out.

And Olivia was the best butterfly by far, finally believing she was indeed

a bright and beautiful star!

Then after the show and the applause of the night, Olivia looked in the mirror and smiled in delight. 'I'm Olivia Catherine Amanda Mae Brown. And I'm free to be me. I may be 'round,' but, I like what I see!"

The Beginning

S.R. Taylor

S.R. Taylor was born to a southern homecoming queen and an air force officer turned preacher. The Taylor family, considered modern day Gypsies, lived all across the United States. She attended seven elementary and nine high schools. Always the new girl, she developed her passion for reading, writing poetry and creating stories while entertaining her younger siblings in the backseat of their ever-traveling station wagon.

As a single mother of two, Taylor continued creating bedtime stories. Night after night, her children urged her to tell 'her funny stories about curious children that looked like them.' She soon discovered she had inherited her father's natural knack of storytelling and found her own unique voice in writing.

Currently her projects include the next installment to the *Free2Bee* series of books—*Harriett Pear Hates Her Hair*. S.R. Taylor is happily-ever-after married and has three children. Her daughter, Athena is the inspiration for *ROUND*.